Alfred and t'
by Brian Trueman

Book version by Nicholas Jon

D0864712

Illustrations from the Cosgrove Hall production
Directed by Chris Taylor

Thames Methuen

First published in Great Britain 1984
by Methuen Children's Books Ltd
11 New Fetter Lane, London EC4P 4EE
in association with Thames Television International Ltd
149 Tottenham Court Road, London W1P 9LL

Printed in Great Britain

ISBN 0 423 01220 7

The unabridged edition of *The Wind in the Willows*
by Kenneth Grahame is available with full colour illustrations
from the award-winning Cosgrove Hall production.

The Cosgrove Hall film of the original book
by Kenneth Grahame is available on Thames Video

Alfred and the Caravan

The autumn promised a good harvest: black-
berries shone from tangles of briars, rowans and
hawthorns were laden, handfuls of elderberries
dangled from sagging branches, and the farmer's
fields were now shimmering gold in the September
sun. Ratty and Mole were to be found, on this
glorious morning, equipped for the road with
knapsacks, sturdy boots and stout sticks, striding
along through the richness. A little way behind,
and *not* striding – indeed resting at the roadside
– was a weary and footsore Toad.

'O, do stop! Do stop!' he pleaded.

'My dear Toad, we stopped two minutes back!' expostulated Rat.

'And two minutes before that!' added Mole.

'Yes, yes! I know! But I can't help it if my wretched straps keep slipping!' Toad argued.

'You shouldn't have tried to carry so much!' Rat retorted.

'So much? There's hardly anything! Smoked salmon, calves' foot jelly, stuffed olives, lemon curd, fruit cake, two peaches, a packet of rich tea biscuits and half a bottle of champagne. I don't call *that* a lot!'

'O, Toad!' His friend's incorrigible impracticality was too much even for the patient Mole. 'If we *keep* stopping, we'll never get anywhere!'

'But we've already got *here*! From *Toad Hall*!'

'My dear Toad, it can't be more than three-quarters of a mile!' Ratty exclaimed in reply.

'Three-quarters of a mile . . . No *wonder* I feel tired! Whoever wanted to go hiking in the first place?'

'You did, Toad!' said Mole, matter-of-factly, over Toad's protestations. ' "Fresh air's the thing," you said!'

'I say – I do dislike a fellow who throws a chap's words back in his face,' replied the unabashed Toad. 'Awfully mean-spirited, I always think!'

The Rat considered. 'Well, Toad, if your new-found enthusiasm for hiking has burnt itself out already, what *do* you want to do?'

'Nothing!' Toad snapped back defiantly.

A new voice joined in. 'That's all as some of us *has* to do!'

Ratty started: 'Hullo! Who's . . .? O! Hullo, Alfred!' And indeed it was Alfred, their faithful companion from the days of the open road and the canary-coloured caravan. Without realising, the three friends had stopped next to the field where he lived, and Alfred had heard them talking through the hedge.

Unlike the Rat, Mole had taken in what Alfred had said. 'All some of us has – er, *have* – to do? How do you mean, Alfred?'

Alfred snorted in reply, and tossed his head towards the next-door field. 'Huh! Hear that!?'

Toad hadn't time for such leisurely discussion – unless it involved him: 'Yes, yes! Sounds like a goods train.' That, come to think of it, was a good cue: 'I say, did I ever tell you . . .'

Alfred wasn't to be diverted: 'Harvester! That's what the noise is. A harvester!'

Rat couldn't see the connection: 'Erm – I don't think . . .'

'It's the farmer! Him an' his new-fangled machines! Ain't good enough to have me pulling the mower like I've always done! He 'as to get a mechanical harvester! Huh!'

Mole was concerned: 'O, dear! So what are you . . .?'

'Nothing! Nothing to do till ploughing starts again! Ain't as if Mr Toad has a caravan for me to pull!'

Toad had forgotten his earlier passion. But caravans had wheels! They were easier than hiking! But he didn't want to give away his motives, and, 'O, yes! The caravan!' was all he allowed himself to say.

Mole was more enthusiastic. 'O, I loved the caravan!' A snatch of their song came back to him: 'It's a life of ease on the Open Road . . .' Rat joined in: 'Rambling where you please on the Open Road . . .' But both stopped short when they heard Alfred remark casually: 'Still there.'

'O, I say, *do* let's see!' Mole was captivated by the prospect. And so was Toad – even if his reasons were a little different. He was determined to demonstrate to his friends just how much he had revelled in those days. 'The journeys we took in her – remember? Those weeks of slothful pleasure?'

The Rat was not to be beguiled. 'No!'

That was not the answer Toad expected. 'Ah ha! Yes, those . . . No! No?'

'You used it for just three days – and then you took up motoring!'

Undaunted by this home-truth, Toad enthused over the abandoned caravan, stuck in a ditch in the corner of the field: 'Ah! See! Here it is! My word, how picturesque it looks!'

Mole was still enraptured in his memories. 'It would be wonderful to travel the open road again!' he enthused.

'Huh! You weren't pulling 'er!' Alfred retorted.

Mole was horrified by his thoughtlessness.
'Oh! No! I'm sorry, Alfred. I forgot!'

But Alfred had been only half-serious in his
complaint. 'Be better'n doing nothing,' he said.

By now, Toad's enthusiasm had been totally
rekindled. 'My friends, we'll do it,' he announced,

She *shall* be restored! We *shall* travel the world –
and not on foot! We *shall* explore the ever-
changing scenery, live the Romany life –'

But he was cut off in the midst of his oratory.
It was the Fieldmice: 'Quick! We'd better get
help! We'll have to . . .' And three of them
scuttled through the hedge from the next-door
field. 'O, Mr Alfred! It's the harvester! It's
mowed our homes!'

Rat and Mole were horrified: 'Mowed your *homes*! Oh my gosh!'

'I knew no good'd come of it!' Alfred remarked gloomily.

'Everything's gone,' bewailed the Fieldmice.

Toad, for all his self-centred talk, was the most generous animal in a crisis – if sometimes a little impractical. 'My poor dear chaps!' he exclaimed. 'Homeless! Well, you'll just have to stay at Toad Hall!'

The Fieldmice were delighted with this ready offer of help, but it wasn't quite the help they needed. 'Please sir, that's very kind of you, but . . . we're not used to *big* houses!'

'*My* house will suit you very well!' Mole asserted.

'Yes, but there isn't just us, Mr Mole!' replied the spokesman.

'How do you mean?' asked the mystified Rat.

'Well, er . . . you see . . .' He whistled through his teeth, and a dozen or so other mice appeared. Mole understood the reason for the Fieldmouse's

hesitation. 'O dear! There wouldn't be room for *half* of them!'

'Not even if some stayed with me!' agreed Rat.

The disappointed Fieldmice broke into a chatter: 'O dear! Whatever shall we do! Nowhere to go! Nowhere to live!' – but they were silenced by Alfred clearing his throat purposefully. 'Ahem!'

'Sorry, Alfred!' Ratty prompted.

'Caravan.'

Mole and Ratty did not immediately follow Alfred's thinking and Mole began, 'I don't think we should be bothering with that when . . .'

'Why can't they stay in it for a while? Just until they find a place of their own.'

'O, Mr Alfred, that would be wonderful!' said the delighted Fieldmice.

'It would have to be mended . . .' Mole put in, his usual practical self.

'Well, we could help you mend it!' said one Fieldmouse, and the others cheered their approval.

'That's jolly decent of you!' Toad enthused, foreseeing some hard work being done for him. 'I say – by this time next week we could be rolling along the open road again!'

Alfred set off to fetch some ropes; Toad began to show the Fieldmice round their new home, extolling its merits like an estate agent with a *particularly* desirable residence. 'It has, of course,

everything you could wish for . . .'
'. . . except a wheel.' Rat interposed quietly.
Toad accepted the prompt, repeated the phrase

– then realised what he'd said. 'Except a *wheel*!?'

'There's one missing! Look!' Rat pointed to the bare axle.

'Please, sir! It's our roundabout,' explained a Fieldmouse. 'It must have come off and rolled onto the roadside, Mr Toad . . .'

'. . . and some of us sit on it, and the others push it round.'

Toad could see his mission. 'Ha! Well now it's going to be a wheel again!' He turned to his friends. 'Leave this to me!' he commanded. Indicating some half of the Fieldmice with a grandiose sweep of his hand, he continued, 'Erm . . .! Ten or a dozen of you mice! Follow me!' And he marched off with his army, just as Alfred returned with the ropes.

So the next hour or so was filled with shouts and cries – of instructions, of effort, of satisfaction as things were done. 'Shall I tie this here?' 'Right, everyone, heave!' 'Look out, young Billy!' And finally, as it came clear 'Hurray!'

Toad, meanwhile, had managed, with much
effort from his little helpers and rather less actual
work from himself, to get the recalcitrant wheel
upright. He attempted to reunite it with the
caravan by rolling it along, like a giant hoop, and
all nearly ended in disaster when it gathered
speed and threatened to run down Toad, who had

somehow contrived to get in front of it. But Mole saved the situation by ramming a stick through the spokes, felling the wheel not too far from where it was needed.

Toad appeared shaken by his experience: 'O dear, O dear!'

Ratty considered. Was Toad really so unnerved by the near-mishap? 'Better catch your breath, Toad,' he remarked, non-commitally, 'before we get back to work.'

'Work? O, yes, of course! Well, now . . .' Toad pulled out his watch. 'Good heavens! Is that the time? I'd no idea! I'll miss my appointment!'

'Appointment, Toad?' said the Rat, suspiciously. 'You never mentioned an appointment!'

'Went clean out of my head! Must rush! I'll . . . er . . . leave my knapsack. Help yourself to lunch! Goodbye!'

'Dear me! *Now* what's he up to? mused Rat, largely to himself. 'No steadiness, that's Toad's trouble! Ah, well, let's get this wheel on.'

After more heaving under Ratty's skilled
direction, the caravan was once more upright
and on four wheels. Rather than leave it in the

draughty corner of the field, Alfred suggested,
they could move to a woodland glade nearby.
That done, they set about cleaning it, and before

long it was restored to its pristine glory.

A week or so later, Ratty and Mole returned, provisions in hand, to prepare the caravan for their promised trip. 'O, Ratty,' Mole remarked enthusiastically as they neared it, 'I am so looking forward to a trip!'

'Yes, I must say that, while an open road will never match a flowing river, I feel a need to travel. It's in the air, y'see. The swallows feel it – they'll soon be flying south.' He broke off, when he saw a line of Fieldmice sitting on the ground beside the caravan with their bags and suitcases, looking as if they were waiting for a charabanc.

'O, hullo!'

'Good morning, Mr Rat! Mr Mole!' they chorused in reply. 'We thought we'd wait – to say "goodbye" and "thank you".'

'Enjoyed your stay, have you?' Mole enquired.

'It's the nicest home that ever was, Mr Mole!'

'Good, good!' Rat approved. 'So where are you making your new home?' he added.

There was an uneasy pause, then one Field-mouse said, tentatively, 'Erm . . . well . . .'

'Look here – you have *found* a new place?' Ratty asked, suspecting that the shy animals, so grateful for the help given to them earlier, might have decided to move on without knowing what awaited them. Mole looked over his glasses, and added, gently, '*Have* you got somewhere?'

'Well . . . not exactly, Mr Mole.'

'Yes or no?' Rat said, more firmly.

'Erm . . . no,' sighed one of the Mice.

'O, my gosh! O, Ratty!' Mole exclaimed, touched both by the Fieldmice's plight and their reluctance to burden others with it.

Rat was already considering what to do: 'Look here, Mole, old fellow – we can't turn these Fieldmice out so that we can have a holiday! They'll be safe and snug here, and we *have* our homes . . . .'

'O, Ratty, I'm so glad you said that!' Mole was eager to agree with his friend's generous gesture. The Rat wondered how to stop the Fieldmice

feeling uneasy at accepting further help. 'Look
here, you fellows – we . . . er . . . we only dropped
by to tell you that it's off,' he said. 'We won't be
going! Important business, and . . . er . . .'

Mole fell in with his friend's deception, and
interrupted: 'That's right! So . . .'

'. . . so you needn't go!' finished Rat.

'You mean we can stay, Mr Rat? That this can always be our home?' said the delighted Field-mice. Rat and Mole nodded. 'O, thank you! Thank you!' the mice chorused their thanks.

But Rat suddenly frowned. 'There's only one thing, Mole.' 'What's that?' 'Toad! He has been going on about the caravan . . .'

'. . . and the Romany life,' Mole concurred, quickly understanding the problem.

'. . . and the open road again,' Ratty added.

'O, dear!' Mole wondered. 'What if he insists . . .?'

'O, Mole!' The Rat was seized by doubt. 'I was too hasty. Perhaps I should have . . .'

Mole was not going to give up, however: 'If we explain to him how things are . . . If we tell him . . .' he began, only to stop, distracted by a tinkling noise. 'Ratty! What's that?'

'I don't know, Mole. It sounds like . . .'

And it was. A bicycle bell – attached to a bicycle, astride which sat . . . Toad! 'Ring-a-ding!

Ring-a-ding! O, for the life a-wheel!' sang the ebullient creature as he rolled into view.

Mole and Rat looked at each other. 'O my!' 'O no!'

Toad shuddered to a halt next to them. 'My dear friends, what joys I have discovered! Behold my wheeled Bucephalus! My Dursley-Pedersen! The finest bicycle that ever was! Such silent, swooping speed! Such hills surmounted, valleys conquered!'

'O Toad! Not another craze!' said Rat, resignedly.

'Craze! Craze! This is but the beginning of a *lifetime's* bliss! Ah, the swift velocipede! To hear the singing of the spokes, the whirr of a well-greased chain . . .'

'Toad!' Ratty attempted to quell Toad's torrent of enthusiasm – to no avail.

'. . . the fresh air streaming past one's face. The whirling kaleidoscope of villages . . .'

'Toad! Do be quiet!' Ratty shouted in desperation.

'O, I say!'

'I thought you wanted to go on a caravan trip!' Rat continued, a trace of irony in his voice, when he'd finally engaged Toad's attention.

'Pooh! Caravan! A snail's home on wheels! A horse-drawn dog-kennel! A mere . . .'

'All right, Toad!' Rat burst in again. 'Am I to take it then that you will *not* be going on a caravan trip?'

For once, Toad realised that his vacillation might irritate his friends, prepared as they evidently were for another trip. But it didn't stop him appealing to them: was it his fault if he had only so recently discovered the delights of two-wheeled transport?

'O, Ratty, Mole – forgive me – but I *cannot* come! I hear the 'ping' of chain-guards, and the ring of bells! I hear . . .'

'*Thank*-you Toad!' said Mole, firmly. 'So the Fieldmice can stay here for a while?'

'Here! Fieldmice? O yes – for ever! No *caravan* is swift enough to match *my* spirit! And now,

dear friends, I must be on my way! The four-
spring patent saddle shall bear me hence! Ting-a-
ling! Farewell!'

'My word,' said Mole, 'he's got it awfully bad!'

'As ever, Mole!' Rat agreed. 'But it won't last.
It never does.'

'Still, the Fieldmice have a home!' Mole
continued, brightening.

'Yes. It's an ill wind that blows nobody any
good, and I must say . . . !'

'Morning all!' a deep voice said cheerfully
behind them. It was Alfred. And he, thought Rat,

would be raring to go. They had forgotten all about him! 'Look, Alfred,' Rat began, 'there's been a change of plan! I'm sorry . . .'

'How did you know that?' Alfred didn't seem downcast – more surprised.

Mole was puzzled. 'How d'you mean, Alfred, "How do *we* know?" How do *you* know?'

'Well – seeing as 'ow it's me who's 'ad to change it . . .'

'*You*?' began Mole. 'But *we* . . .'

'It's the 'arvester,' Alfred explained. 'Broken down it has! Blew up, it has! Ha, ha! Farmer's real mad! So he 'as to turn to me, like. I'm . . . sorry to spoil your plans!'

'Not at all, Alfred! Not at all!' Mole said, smiling inwardly.

As Alfred trotted off to work, muttering about new-fangled rubbish, Mole turned to Rat. 'Well! So that's all right! Toad doesn't care, Alfred can't come, the Fieldmice have a home, and we . . .' He hesitated, a little sad at losing the prospect he'd been so looking forward to.

'. . . we have our homes to go to!' said Rat brightly, then added, 'Wouldn't fancy a day on the river, I suppose?'

'O, Ratty!' said Mole, contentedly.